SEaDOG

Claire Saxby

illustrated by Tom Jellett

RANDOM HOUSE AUSTRALIA

For Mark, David, Paul and Andrew: Seadogs one and all – C.S.

For Milly and Zoe – T.J.

RANDOM HOUSE AUSTRALIA

A Random House book
Published by Random House Australia Pty Ltd
Level 3, 100 Pacific Highway, North Sydney NSW 2060
www.randomhouse.com.au

First published by Random House Australia in 2013
This edition published in 2014

Text copyright © Claire Saxby 2013
Illustration copyright © Tom Jellett 2013

The moral right of the author and illustrator has been asserted.

All rights reserved. No part of this book may be reproduced or transmitted by any person or entity, including
internet search engines or retailers, in any form or by any means, electronic or mechanical, including photocopying
(except under the statutory exceptions provisions of the Australian *Copyright Act 1968*), recording, scanning or by any
information storage and retrieval system without the prior written permission of Random House Australia.

Addresses for companies within the Random House Group can be found at www.randomhouse.com.au/offices

National Library of Australia
Cataloguing-in-Publication Entry

Author: Saxby, Claire
Title: Seadog / Claire Saxby; Tom Jellett, illustrator
ISBN: 978 1 74275 651 6 (pbk)
Target Audience: For primary school age
Subjects: Dogs – Juvenile fiction
Other Authors/Contributors: Jellett, Tom
Dewey Number: A823.4

Cover and internal design by Tom Jellett and
Julie Thompson at Penny Black Design
Printed and bound in China by Everbest Printing Pty Ltd

Our dog is not a work dog,
a round-'em-bring-'em-home dog.

Our dog is a

SEADOG,

a run-and-scatter-
gulls dog.

Our dog is not a fetch dog,

a chase-and-bring-
the-stick dog.

Our dog is a
SEADOG,

a crunch-and-
munch-and-
chew dog.

Our dog is not
a trick dog,

a sit-still-then-
roll-over dog.

Our dog is a

SEADOG,

a jump-and-chase-
the-waves dog.

Our dog is not
a clean dog,

a shiny

or a fluffy dog.

Our dog is a
SEADOG,

a find-and-roll-in-fish dog.

Pee-ee-euw, SEADOG!

Bath time!

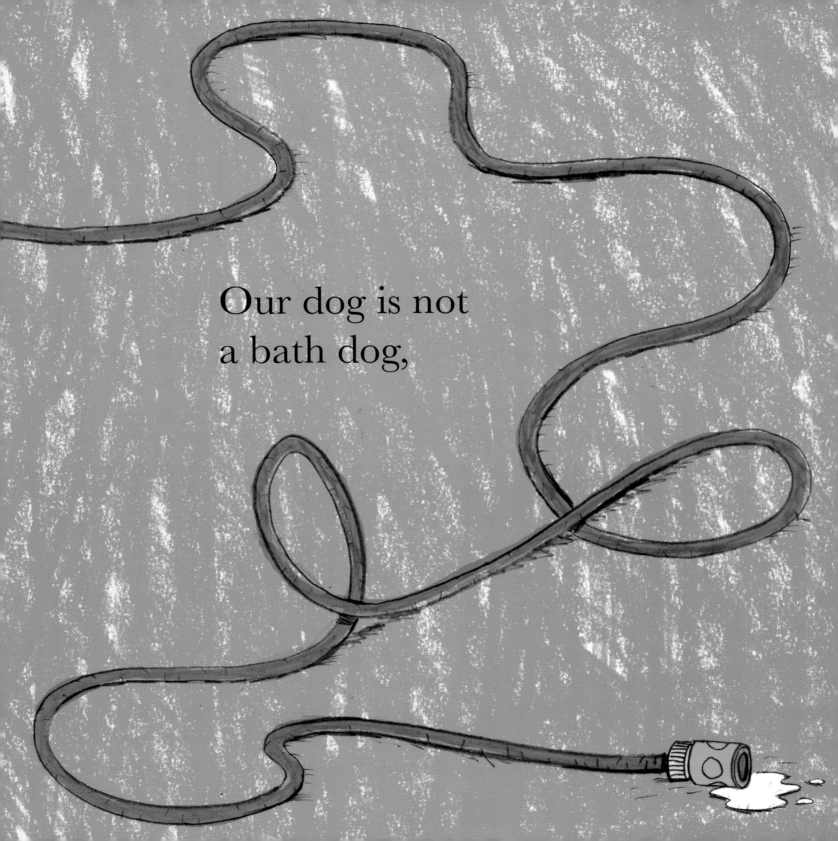

Our dog is not
a bath dog,

a love-the-soap-and-suds dog.

Our dog is a
SEADOG,

and seadogs don't like baths.

But even seadogs seem to know,

that some things must be so,

and for a few minutes,
a few short minutes,
our dog, our seadog,

our race-waves-like-the-wind dog,

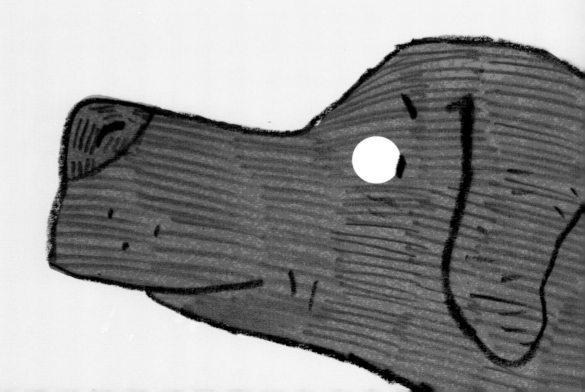

becomes a
sit-still-till-it's-done dog.

Now, our dog is a clean dog,

a shiny and a fluffy dog,

until someone opens the door…